didn't ring

MICHAEL I

MIND the GAP

ILLUSTRATED BY

CAROLINE HOLDEN

adlib... Scholastic Publications Limited

crazeeee

Scholastic Children's Books,
Scholastic Publications Ltd,
7-9 Pratt Street, London NW1 OAE, UK

Scholastic Inc., 730 Broadway,
New York, NY 10003, USA

Scholastic Canada Ltd, 123 Newkirk Road,
Richmond Hill, Ontario, Canada L4C 3G5

Ashton Scholastic Pty Ltd, PO Box 579,
Gosford, New South Wales, Australia

Ashton Scholastic Ltd, Private Bag 1,
Penrose, Auckland New Zealand

First published in the UK by Scholastic Publications Ltd, 1992
Text Copyright © 1992 by Michael Rosen
Ilustrations Copyright © 1992 by Caroline Holden

ISBN 0 590 54009 2

Designed by Ness Wood

Printed in Great Britain by The Bath Press, Avon

TELLY STAR

The first time I was ever asked on telly
was a complete disaster.

When ITV first started up
their children's TV had this brilliant original idea
of having a programme where two guys and a woman
sit around in a studio with a dog and a parrot
making gliders and icing cakes
or go and parachute off the Eiffel Tower
to raise money for blind rabbits in Indonesia.
Really original.
It was called Magpie
and they asked me to come on there
when my first book, 'Mind Your Own Business' came out.

I went there in the morning
and we spent all day rehearsing what I had to say.
The idea was that the woman presenter was going to say:
Hallo and welcome to Magpie
and on the programme we've got a real live poet
and he's just written a book.
What's your book called, Mike?

And I was going to say
Mind Your Own Business.

A Joke.

We rehearsed this over and over again, all day.

What's your book called?
Mind Your Own Business.

Somewhere around tea-time
they all started rushing about and sweating
and someone told me I wasn't going to sit on a chair
I would have to sit on a kind of green platform
and on the platform was this little wobbly plastic
mushroom
for me to sit on.
Trouble was:
when I tried to sit on it
it was smaller than my bum
and it felt like I was going to fall off it
AND the platform.

While I was trying to get the hang of it
this bloke starts shouting:
Standby everyone, here goes
and he starts counting backwards:
10,9,8,7...
So I'm thinking
why's this bloke counting backwards at the top of his
voice
all of a sudden?
And why am I trying to sit on a little plastic mushroom?
Then the bloke presenter leans across to me
does a big thumbs-up and a wink
and says:
Four million watching this, Mike.
It's going out live.

Panic:
Live? Live? I didn't know it was live.
What if I make a mistake or something?

Wobble wobble wobble on the mushroom
then the bloke who was counting backwards
stops:
6,5,4 -

he's stopped.
Why's he stopped?
He's forgotten how to count backwards.
I turn and look at him to say:
Er it goes 3,2,1 actually.

But then all the lights changed.
Why have the lights changed?
Wobble wobble wobble on the plastic mushroom

then the woman presenter turned into a chicken.

She started nodding and smiling and clucking
and blinking her eyes
and quivering her lips:
Hallo, blink quiver
welcome to Magpie cluck blink.

So I turn and stare at her:
why's she doing that?
Is this supposed to be sexy?

And she goes on:
...And on the programme today we've got a real live poet

and he's just written a book.
What's your book called, Mike?

AND I FORGOT THE NAME OF MY BOOK

I just went: Er er ...

So she starts up all over again
with the clucking and the blinking
and I'm still wobbling on the mushroom
and wondering why that bloke couldn't count backwards
and four million people are watching this

and she has another go:
And what's your book called, Mike?

Well, it's er called Mind Your Own Business

I RUINED THE GAG
I BLEW IT.
It was a complete disaster.

But the weird thing about telly
is that you don't know it's a disaster.
I thought I had been great
and I dashed home
burst through the front door
opened out my arms:
DER-DANNNNN...HOW WAS I?

And everyone looked the other way and went:
mmm, yeah, well, mmmm...

GRAMMAR

The teacher said:
A noun is a naming word.
What is the naming word in the sentence:
'He named the ship LUSITANIA'?
'Named', said George.
Wrong, it's 'ship'.
Oh, said George.

The teacher said:
A verb is a doing word.
What is the doing word in the sentence:
'I like doing homework'?
'Doing', said George.
Wrong, it's 'like'.
Oh, said George.

The teacher said:
An adjective is a describing word.
What is the describing word in the sentence
'Describing sunsets is boring'?
'Describing', said George.
Wrong, it's 'boring'.
I know it is, said George.

7

Solomon the Cat

I was 7
There was a competition in the paper
It was: Write a story
and the best story would be printed.

I thought I'd go for it.

So I'm sitting there with my paper
and I'm thinking of this book I read at school about
Solomon the Cat
and Solomon gets thrown out
and goes from house to house
asking for somewhere to be put up.

So I think:
I could write a story like that:
I called it:
Solomon the Cat
and I wrote how
Solomon gets thrown out

and goes from house to house
asking for somewhere to be put up.
I sent it in and I won the competition
and it was printed in the paper.

Solomon the Cat
by Michael Rosen
aged 7 and threequarters.
My mum and dad were very pleased with me.

It got printed in the paper's Christmas annual too.

Solomon the Cat,
by Michael Rosen
aged 7 and threequarters.

Some time later we got a letter from the paper
saying they'd heard from someone who said
theyd bought a children's picture book
about a cat called Solomon
who gets thrown out
and goes from house to house
asking for somewhere to be put up.

olomon the Cat
y Michael Rosen
aged 7$\frac{3}{4}$

See this, Con, my dad says to my mum,
see this? Someone's stolen Mick's story
and made a book out of it.
Would you believe it? The things people do.
If I had the time I'd try and get hold of that book
and sue the pants off them.
No,no,I said, I shouldn't bother, it was ages ago.

Not long ago, I got a letter from a girl in America.
She said she'd won a State Poetry Competition
judged by the poet, John Ciardi.
She'd won with a poem that went:
Down behind the dustbin
I met a dog called Jim
He didn't know me
and I didn't know him.
You wrote that poem,
 Mr Rosen, she said,
and now they want to print it
in the paper,
what shall I do?

I sent her a letter back and said:
Don't worry. I know someone
who once wrote a story called:
Solomon the Cat
who gets thrown out
and goes from house to house . . .

And now the Weather Forecast ...

Good evening
many of you will have experienced
outbreaks of some pretty bad programmes
in the last 24 hours
with some rather unpleasant ones earlier in the day.

In the next twelve hours things are unlikely to get any
better
and we expect programmes to be dull everywhere
with the odd funny interval perhaps popping up later on.
Here's the satellite picture:
terrible conditions moving in from America
almost certain to hit all regions
soon.

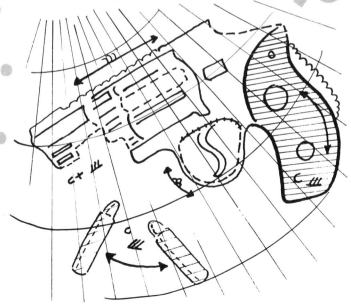

Primary School Intro

I won't introduce you, Mr Rosen, I'll just say a few
words.
Good Morning everyone...

I think you could have done that with a bit of a smile,
couldn't you?
No, don't do it again.
On your bottoms on the back row.
On your bottoms.
Now,
we've got someone to visit us today, haven't we?
Someone very special.
Someone who's come a very long way
and here he is.
Do you know who he is?
Yes?
No - it's not Michael Jackson
he's in America
and anyway he's .... a singer.
Yes it's Michael Rosen
and what does Michael Rosen do?
He's a ....
no, Lee
a bookmaker is something very different.
He's an author.
What did you say Christine?
No, dear, your father's name's not 'author', it's Arthur.
Yes Susan?
Well, we don't normally ask people

how much money they get
as soon as we meet them, do we?
(I'm so sorry, Mr Rosen
they are very forthright, the children round here.)
Now let's get on.
This is Michael Rosen and he writes books,
and he's going to -
Rasheda, where are you going?
I'd much prefer it if you asked-
and you *have* had all playtime to do it in, haven't you?
On your bottoms, on the back row, on your bottoms.
Mr Rosen is tall enough for all of you to see him.
Richard, that isn't what we say
if we see someone with a beard, is it?
(He didn't mean to be rude, Mr Rosen,
but he hasn't got a father
and I'm afraid he calls all men with beards, 'Hairyface'
you can ask Mr Hogan)
You-
Let go of Tariq's ear
yes you
who *are* you?
you don't go to this school, do you?
I'm so sorry Mr Rosen
we seem to have a stranger in our midst.
Well, if he goes to Morningtown
that's where he ought to be.
Well,
if he hasn't got a teacher today
then he ought to be at home.
Well,

13

if his mum and dad are out
then he ought to be...
well
he ought not to be here.

Everybody
SIT DOWN
on your bottoms.
On your bottoms
settle down
sett-le
sett-le.

Mr Rollo
I wonder if I could ask you to pop into the kitchen
and ask Mrs Argyle
if they could just possibly stop banging the saucepans
for the next minute or so.
No, David
we won't all pretend to bang saucepans
and Samantha's head isn't the saucepan
you're going to bang.
(They do a lot of making their own music here, you
know)
On your bottoms everyone
you've all seen David and Samantha before.
All eyes to the front.
To the front.
The front.

Now let's all have a really nice time

14

and when we laugh
let's just laugh
and not do what we did
when Wizzo the Wizard came, eh? Wayne? Darren?
Hong?
Let's show Mr Rosen
we know how to behave ourselves
like sensible grown up boys and girls.

Now, Tariq's friend,
where's he gone?
Ah - you had better come with me
I'm so sorry Mr Rosen
I can't stay to see you
I've got to see a mother
about a girl who swallowed a marble.
Her brother wants the marble back.

So settle down everyone
(they're all yours, Mr Rosen)

This way boy - what did you say your name was?

(I mustn't keep you any longer, Mr Rosen.
If they start banging the saucepans again
Mr Rollo will deal with it.

They're all yours, Mr Rosen.
I'm sure they'll be a very good audience.)

SHLUMP

Mum doesn't often shout at me
but when she's fed up with me
she goes in for great long speeches
and she doesn't hear anything you say

she says:
I'm tired of seeing you in those trousers
why don't you go to the men's shop in the High Street?
What's it called?
Harry Boothroyds?

No, Mum, one's called Harry Reed
and the other's called John Booth

... or you could go and see the little man under the
bridge
and he'd fit you up with a nice pair of trousers.
That Harry Boothroyd he has ...

No, Mum
one's called Harry Reed
and the other's called John Booth

... he's got nice trousers
you look a complete shlump in those trousers
I'd give you the money
you could go to Harry Boothroyd's tomorrow ...
No, Mum
one's called Harry Reed

and the other's called John Booth
... you could look smart
those trousers are a disgrace
I'm ashamed to see you wearing them
I'm sure the Stollar boy
doesn't wear trousers like that
doesn't he get his trousers at Harry Boothroyd's?

He gets his trousers at Harry Reed's or John Booth's,
Mum

... so what's the matter with you?
Don't you want to look smart?
All this don't-care-what-I-look-like stuff
where do you get it from?
You don't see me going about looking untidy
- your father maybe -
but even he goes and gets himself
a couple of suits at Harry Boothroyd's

No Mum,
Harry Reed or John Booth's

... I'm giving you the money.
Here. Go now
and don't come back
until you've got yourself a pair of trousers
I can't bear looking at you another minute ...

Which one shall I go to Mum?
Harry Reed or John Booth's?

How should I know? I haven't heard of either of them.

Is it or isn't it

Maybe what I write aren't poems
maybe this isn't a poem
the only way we can find out if this is a poem
is to find an expert
do we have an expert here?
We need someone to tell us
if this has got the right qualifications
to be a poem.
If it hasn't
then it should be put in the bin marked:
'Bin-for-things-we-experts-
haven't-got-a-name-for-yet-
but-very-soon-will'.

If this **IS** a poem
then it should be put in the bin marked:
'Bin-for-things-waiting-for-experts-
to-give-a-mark-out-of-20-for'.

If this isn't a poem
but looks as if it is pretending to be one
it is a generally held view by most reputable experts
you should stop reading it
straightaway.

HISTORY

Our school caretaker
was called Mr Tyrell.

Doing history helped me deal with him.

We learnt when we were 7
that 800 years ago
the king was William II.
He was shot through the heart
with a bow and arrow
by someone called Tyrell.

Every time I saw Mr Tyrell
after that
I always did a quick check
to make sure
he wasn't carrying anything long and
springy.
But just in case I missed it
I always had my hands up in front of me
at the ready
to guard myself.

Lucky we did history at school
otherwise
I might have a bad chest.

School Visit

The name tag on her pinny says, Patricia Kaufpisch.
I'm going to ask her if she knows what it means ...
her father must have told her ...
no, her father didn't tell her...
no, I can't tell her in front of her friends...
I've got to say why they called her Kaufpisch...
maybe I will tell her that old Germanic joke...

there were these Jews, right?
living in Germany about 200 years ago, right?
and they were called ben This and ben That,
so these Germans said to the Jews
if you want to be citizens of Germany
you got to have German names, right?

but it'll cost you...
and if you haven't got much money
(money, Jews, gettit?)
you'll have to buy ones like
Ochsenschwanz, Eselkkopf, Saumagen and
Hinkedigger:
Oxprick, Asshead, Pigbelly, and Cripple...
so this Jew comes up to the German in charge of names
and he says, I've come to buy a name for myself
have you got any of those pretty ones?
Rosenthal, Valley-of-the-roses, that sort of thing?
Sure, says the man in charge,
but Valley-of-the-roses doesn't come cheap,
what sort of money are we talking about here?
Oh I've hardly got two coins to rub together,
says the Jew.
So what do you do for a living, son? says the man in
charge.
I sell things, a bit of this, a bit of that.
Fair enough, says the man in charge, fair enough.
How's this for size? Kaufpisch, Sellpiss.

...if I could talk to her on her own, I could tell her
but she's saying , Goodbye thank you for talking to us,
Mr Rosen.
Rosen? It means roses.
So? I was one of the lucky ones.

21

The Bantu and the Mbuti

(from Maurice Godelier:
'The Mental and the Material')

For the Bantu
the forest is hostile inhospitable and deadly
they venture only rarely into its depths
and always at great risk
as for them it is peopled
by demons
evil spirits
and Mbuti.

For the Mbuti
the forest holds no secrets
they easily and quickly find their bearing there
the forest holds in its depths
all the animals and plants they need
in order to survive in the forest
they are protected from the sun
and the springs are plentiful and pure
they see the game that they catch
and the produce they gather
as gifts lavished upon them
by the forest.

For the Mbuti
the open spaces cleared by the Bantu
seem hostile
a place where the heat is overwhelming
the water polluted and deadly
and illnesses are numerous.

For the Bantu
the forest is in the way
it must be cleared with axes
if manioc and maize are to be cultivated
a Bantu does not know the forest well
and rarely ventures into its depths
for fear of getting lost
and dying there.

VICTORIA STATION

Time to catch the
8.32 train to Brighton
The time is 8.50
300 people waiting
in front of the notice board
wondering where their train is . . .

'DEPARTURE INFORMATION'???
blank blank blank

'VICTORIA TRAIN SERVICE
INFORMATION'???
closed

'CUSTOMER INFORMATION'???
'Welcome to London Victoria'

LOUDSPEAKER???
'The trab dom flapnong pip
diz the platefoftee
for Free Ditches shopping
tat Cratpick, Bombtee and Free Ditches . . .'

300 people waiting

ONE

one bloke
one Suzuki
one cylinder
one spark plug
one journey
one a.m.
thousands driven crazeeeeee

To Hull

I was on a train to Hull
and this bloke turned to me and said
Come on kill me
And I said
I'm sorry I don't think I can.
And he said
Come on kill me
And I said
I'm not in the mood
And he said
You come to kill me
    and I go for me knife stuck down me sock
    and so you see me bend
    and you come for me
    but I flip you over me shoulder
    and stab you ...
    come on kill me.
I said
Not now, people are watching.
And he said,
Trained, I am.
    Commando.
    Been sitting in the desert
    in Australia
    for 3 bloody years

And then on the coast.
Got so bored
I used to take pot shots
at passing ships.
Trained I am.
I could kill you in five seconds
with me bare hands
you come for me
I'm up there
with the back of me hand
then in there
and you're just a slab of meat.
I said
Mmmmmmm
He said
What are you? Some kind of bum?
I said
Sort of.
He said
I'm free now.
   free at last
   free at last
   free at bloody last
   three bloody years, he said
and started crying.

27

Dirty Book

They had this second-hand book sale for Oxfam
at school, and I turned up late.
There weren't many books left,
so I wasn't going to hang about long
when this crazy guy called Nig says
- Come over here, there's some great books here.

He had a row of beat-up old paperbacks
that looked like they'd been used to dry the dishes
with
-'s OK, Nig, don't fancy the look of any of them.
So then this Nig starts dancing about
with one of these books in his hand.
- You've never read anything like this one,
    see this woman on the cover, she's French,
    and it's during the war,
    and she's in the Resistance, OK?
    And look at her, man, look at her
    once those Germans get hold of her
    can you imagine? Can you imagine what goes on?
    And it's all in here, man,
    she's the one telling it.
    What do you say? Do you want it?

- It doesn't look like that kind of book
    from the cover, I said,
    she's just standing there.
So now he grabs me by the arm and mutters in my
ear
- of course they can't show that kind of stuff on the
    cover,

it's much too hot, COME on buy it, man
You'll thank me for this one, I tell you.
So I bought it, took it home, hid it under my bed,
didn't want to get caught reading dirty books
didn't want them to find out
that I wanted to read about Germans and
French Resistance women.
Some of their friends had been in the Resistance.
My father sang French Resistance songs.
This was really filthy stuff I was getting down to here
and I knew it.

So then I read it.
Slowly
carefully
page by page
no jumping
no reading ahead.
Every now and then
it seemed like there would be
some of the kind of stuff
Nig was on about ...
I turned the page and
nothing
not a word
I was furious.

Back at school I went up to this Nig guy and told him,
- That book was nothing like what you said.
- I'm not surprised, he said, I haven't read it.
- So why did you give me all that rubbish about it?
- So you'd buy it, of course,
   it was all for Oxfam, wasn't it?
   You didn't waste your money, did you?

29

Flight Problem

The most uncomfortable thing that can happen to you
on an aeroplane is not turbulence, it's flatulence.

Happened to me once,
I had a drunk one side of me, a nun the other.
You think you can make the fart go back inside
but it keeps coming back.
It says, Hi, it's me again. How you doing?

Get back you fool.
Can't you see I'm sitting next to a nun?

Then it starts to hurt. Horrible cramps.
There's only one thing for it: to the toilet.

Get up and start to climb over the nun,
but it takes quite a bit of effort ...
so whoosh, back it comes, rushing to say hallo:
it's me again, hello everybody.

Get back. Don't talk to the nun.
She doesn't want to talk to you.

I just manage to keep it away from talking to her.
Down to the toilet
OK, you can come out now.
Silence.

OK you can come out now.
Silence.
I start jumping up and down.
Nothing.

It's obviously very fussy about where it likes to be seen.
It will not come out.
So back to my seat.
Climb over the nun, sit down and it's ...

Hello again, it's me, where's that nice lady
in the black and white outfit?
I'd like a word with her before we land ...

C

I was crazy about C.
all summer I chased
I said I liked her earrings
appeared in her doorway
stood in her room
stretched my legs
nothing so large or loud
had been there before
her mouth opened
she said yes

come autumn
there was a danger
I was something
she might be ashamed of
her mouth closed
and I went off on the back seat of a Ford

Ruby

Ruby
who didn't have children
used to tell us about things that happened to her.
She was a teacher, and she said she took a class
of fourteen year olds to Switzerland
and everywhere they went there was a boy in her
group
who kept saying in a deadly glum voice:
It's not as good as South Harrow Gasworks.

When Ruby took them up in the ski-lift, he said,
It's not as good as South Harrow Gasworks.
When she took them to see the glacier, he said,
It's not as good as South Harrow Gasworks.
When she took them to see the giant jet of water
by the side of Lake Geneva, he said,
It's not as good as South Harrow Gasworks.

I suspect that so far,
this story has very little significance to you.
You probably don't care very much about the
Gasworks, South Harrow.
As it happens I was born in a room that looked
out on some gasworks.
In actual fact, though I don't want to make a fuss
about it,
they were the
South Harrow Gasworks.

The day she found a condom in her son's coat pocket
the day she found a condom in her son's coat pocket
was a
disaster.

CONDOM

The neighbours were appalled.
They said:
Mrs F found a condom in T's coat pocket.
Mrs F?
Uh huh ... in T's coat pocket.

The neighbours were also sympathetic:
Oh poor you, Mrs F
such a shock
so unexpected
in T's coat pocket.

CONDOM

The friends giggled:
You know what happened to T and his mum?
She found a condom in his coat pocket?
Which one?
You mean which condom?
No, which pocket?

CONDOM

The mother took action:
kept him indoors at all times except in school hours,
cut off all his purchasing power,
stopped all allowances, pocket money and Saturday jobs
which explains why

40 weeks after the time a relief teacher didn't turn up
a close friend of T gave birth to a lovely little girl.

W.H. Smith

Victoria Station
rush hours:

Some are grabbing at the evening paper.
Some are loitering among the Bargain Books:
Great Motorways of the World
reduced to £3.50.

Over there
a row of silent clean men stand side by side
face to the wall, heads bowed,
staring at pages and pages of
bent and stretched bits of women.

Later at home
will it be cauliflower cheese again?
And that moment of tenseness with the 14
year old ...
'... doesn't suit you ... it'll give boys ideas ...'

Father

Sometime after my mum died
my dad rang me up and said
he'd like to come over and have a chat
and I said fine, anytime, you know that.

So he came over and he seemed a bit twitchy
he kept running his finger under his collar
but it was nice seeing him talking about some new book
and a terrific Italian film
but he didn't seem to have anything particular on his mind
until it was time for him to go
and instead of me just saying goodbye to him at the door
and him disappearing down the dark stairs on his own
and me going back into my room wondering
how he was making out on his own
especially as he always used to say
he was such bad company for himself ...
instead, he said,
come down with me to the car,
I've something I want to talk to you about.

So I said, fine, of course,
and I couldn't think what it was,
maybe he was selling up and going to live in Canada
or maybe he was really ill and
we'd have to go through all that awful stuff again
sometimes bad luck runs in streaks
and I wish like hell he'd give up smoking
he managed when Mum was ill, didn't he?

but it was nice

seeing him

I want to talk

to you about.

36

So by now, we'd got downstairs and he says,
get into the car
and I can see he's really worried now
cos he's got that frowny smile going
and he's breathing fairly deep
makes him look a bit younger
and he says, look I'm going to find this really difficult
to say to you, Mick ...
and now I'm thinking he's going to say one of those
nice flattering things he sometimes says to me
about something I've done
how it was nice that I did come and live in with them
when she was dying ...
but then he says -
- I'm getting married.

So I say,
that's great, who is she?
And he says,
hang on, hang on, don't you mind?
And I said,
mind? Why should I mind?
And he says,
Well I knew you were always very close to Connie,
    and I just thought ...
And I said,
how could I mind? It's nothing to do with me,
And he said
of course it's to do with you.
And I said

well I'm telling you I don't mind, but who is she?
And he said,
phew, that's a load off my mind, I can tell you,
    you can't imagine how relieved I am.
And I said,
good, but who is she?
And he said,

are you really sure

are you really sure you don't mind?
I said,
I'm really really sure.

you don't min

And he said,
Well you don't know her ...
So I said
well done, wow what a surprise.

And you really don't mind, he says,
Of course I don't, I say.
You'll meet her soon, he says.

I did
but he didn't invite me to the wedding, did he?
The old sod.

did he.

Swallows

The notice said:
Only swallows in a distressed condition
can be taken to Mrs McGrath.

Did this mean that robins, thrushes, eagles
and other birds in a distressed condition
could not be taken to Mrs McGrath?

Or did it mean that
you had to take all the swallows that weren't distressed
to somebody else like Mrs Lafferty or Mr Rabinovitz
but not Mrs McGrath?

Or did it mean that
Mrs McGrath was getting fed up with being given
ordinary healthy swallows all the time
but found it more interesting and stimulating
to receive distressed ones?

Or did it mean that
you could take distressed swallows to Mrs McGrath
but all other swallows had to get there
under their own steam?

to Mrs McGrath, as the crow flies...

A

When I was going out with A. I had this idea
I could come and see her in the middle of the night
if she made sure to leave her window open.
She said she wasn't sure it was a good idea
so I said, Oh.
She said, 'But I'll leave my window open anyway'.
I turned up at 12.30, climbed through the window
took my clothes off and got into bed.
About five minutes later, we heard her dad going to bed
but suddenly his footsteps started getting nearer.
I jumped out of bed and jumped into her cupboard
and stood there, starkers.
He came in.
You still awake, dear? he said.
Mmmmm, she said.
You all right? he said.
Mmm mm, she said.
You're not worried about your A-levels, are you?
No.
School OK?
Mmm mm
You're not cold with the window open like that?
It's OK.
Goodnight then, love.

Night, Dad.
And he went out.
I came out of the cupboard.
**She said she thought it was a bit risky
me hanging about.**
I said I didn't know about it being risky
it was certainly bloody cold.

So I got dressed and
climbed back out the window.

'But I'll leave the
window open anyway.'

The black ticket collector was fifty.
 When he swore to tell the whole truth etc
 he looked at the Book like he knew it off by heart.

His lawyer said
the three white boys tried to run through the barrier
   without paying.
When the ticket collector stopped them they started to
   beat him up.
But he grabbed two of the boys, put them in the broom
   cupboard
chased off up the road, caught the third
and locked him in the broom cupboard, too.

The boys' lawyer had an Oxford college in his mouth
and trundled out the law court patter:
- Rather than events being as you describe
  I would suggest that you chose to assault these three
    boys
  I would suggest that you bore a grudge against them
  I would suggest that you took it upon yourself to attack
    them.
  and I would suggest -
The ticket collector had never heard the I-would-suggest
  game
played by lawyers, believed by no one.
Furious, he called out:
- And I would suggest to you, sah,
  that as you was not present at de time
  you know nottin at ahl abote it.

The judge flipped up his glasses
- Very good very good. What d'you say to that?
And the lawyer said:
- ber ber ber ber
and went into a speedy decline.

PRESENTING

Cecil Rhodes, John Hawkins, Captain Cook, Oliver
Cromwell,
Lord Clive, Lord Codrington
and a cast of millions
in the
GREAT ILLEGAL IMMIGRANT SHOW!

Gasp with amazement at
Cecil Rhodes' frantic grabbing of African lands.
Be stunned to silence
as you watch the Matabele forced to sign away
all rights to everything of where they live.

Gape with wonder at John Hawkins'
breathtaking kidnap of African people
and then before your very eyes
sell them like horses.
You'll hardly believe your ears
listening to Captain Cook
beating his diseased sailors to pulp
to help him take over the South Seas.

Sit riveted in your seats
as
Oliver Cromwell
the founder of our parliament

forbids the Irish to speak Irish
and then exiles them from Ireland.

You'll think your eyes deceive you
as
you watch the great East India Company
milk the richest nation in the world
till its fields lie dry
and millions lie dying from hunger.

Hold on to your seats as you are transfixed
by
the noble Codrington in Barbados
trying to breed slaves to cut his sugar cane
and clean his palace.

All these and many more:
wiping out Indians in America
Aborigines in Australia
Scots in Scotland
in
THE SEVEN GREAT PLUNDERS OF THE
WORLD
in
THE GREAT ILLEGAL IMMIGRANT SHOW

Still running ...

test match CRICKET

My mother didn't play cricket,
never watched it
ignored all talk of ashes, ducks and maidens.
In the middle of August she took less interest
in Test Matches than the cat.

Yet when she knew she was dying
and was probably weighing up
the having of children
losing one
reading her way out of the slums
discovering she was someone
people travelled to listen to

she said
I've had a good innings, haven't I?

At Easter things got pretty serious at our school.
Before the event there was an enormous amount
of hymn practice and when we sang:
There is a green hill far away
Without a city wall ...
every year they told us
that it doesn't mean
that the green hill hasn't got a wall.

Then we went back to class and they told us the story:
those horrible Jews getting him
and poor old Pontius Pilate not knowing what to do
and then hammering nails through his hands and feet
then afterwards with him wandering down the street
and Thomas sticking his fingers
into this bleeding hole in his side ...
the whole thing was pretty serious and pretty messy.

I felt a bit bad about those Jews.
I mean I didn't think Zeyda*'d do a thing like that
and I kept my head down in class
in case anyone thought I was in on it too.
But as Jesus was a Jew as well
I didn't see why I should get it in the neck.

As for Pontius Pilate, I found out later
he was really like any other ordinary Roman psychopath
and loved stringing people up,
especially Jews.
Strange story -
a bit too violent for kids, I should think.

(*Yiddish for Grandfather)

ARSENAL

When I go to watch Arsenal at Highbury
there's a bloke there
who cheers Arsenal's black players on:
Come on, Rocky, go for it, Michael Thomas
lovely ball, Paul

but when the other team's got black players
he shouts:
Black bastard, gettim.

Grace

At the end of my first week at Tyneholme
Nursery School
Miss Hornby met my mother at the door
and asked her if she'd prefer it if I didn't say
grace before meals.
- No, Michael can say grace, my mother said.
So, Miss Hornby said,
- It's just that we ask the children to stand,
  close their eyes and put their hands together
  and we say, thank you God for what we are
about to receive,
  but Michael sits down in his seat and shouts:
  No thank you god, no thank you god.

My mother said she would speak to me.

I was soon knuckling down to grace
and went on to say it at school for years.

My mother told me this story
but never explained how she managed
to get me to do something she didn't believe in.

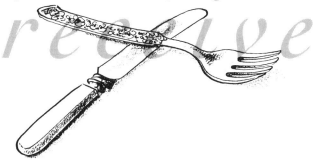

MAD
ABOUT
HEALTH

I eat carrots
I eat cabbage
I eat sprouts
I eat radish

don't eat sugar
don't eat fat
what about salt?
don't eat that

look after myself
I'm mad about health
mad about health
mad about myself

I go for a jog
I go for a swim
I go for a run
I go to the gym

I got the gear
I got the kit
got the strip
it's a perfect fit

look after myself
I'm mad about health
mad about health
mad about myself

feel my pulse rate
feel my biceps
feel my kneecap
feel my triceps
I'm really fit
but d'you know what?
my right knee
hurts a lot.

right knee's swollen
ankle's sprained
wrist is twisted
shoulder's strained

but I'm really fit
I'm much stronger
never mind the pain
I'm gonna live longer

something funny
I've been told
why work so hard
just to get old?

I don't get that
not at all
can't stop now
gotta do some more

look after myself
I'm mad about health
mad about health
mad about myself

no time left
to hang about
no time left
for going out
no time left
to see the wife
I don't care
I'm fit for life
that's what I am
fit for life

pity about the knee
I'm fit for life
pity about the ankle
I'm fit for life
pity about the wife
I'm fit for life.

Then

I was there

and saw my mother sit up

her bones pushing at her skin

reach forward

and fingertip Susanna's swelling belly:

wished her an easy time

good things for the child

didn't let on she knew

she'd be gone

by the time the child swam out

breathed

and eyed the light

swelling belly

how
many

how many people
who know,
don't say?

how many people
who say,
don't say it all?

how many people
who say it all,
don't get heard?

how many people
who get heard
get rubbed out?

how many people
who get rubbed out,
get forgotten?

how many people
remember the ones
they want us to forget?

53

At the Traffic Lights

Tall Sikh, about 60, with stick, walking north
Group of boys, in school uniform, walking south
They pass the Sikh.
One, clean, smart in school uniform turns
hurls an apple at the Sikh.

The man flinches, grabs his head.
Before he turns, the boy has whisked back
and now larks about with his mates.
When the man finally swivels round
he stares through his glasses
but all he sees is a crowd.

He stands now leaning on his stick
looking.

All this I saw through the windscreen of my car.
The lights changed.
I couldn't call the boy back.

I've called him back here.
What shall I ask him?
And what can I say to the man?

Mother

When my dad burps really loudly
my mum says
Was that nice? Was that necessary?

When I put my finger in my ear
my mum says
Don't pick it, wash it.

When she can't find my dad
my mum says
Ask your father what he's doing
and tell him to stop it.

When the dishwasher breaks down
my mum says the plate's in the wishdasher.

When I complain about doing the washing-up
my mum says
let self-sacrifice be its own reward.

Meeting

she wrote to him saying
she was travelling north

he thought he could hitch lifts
for five hundred miles
and be at the station to surprise her

she thought
she'd be seeing him in England

he made it
and slept in the waiting room
while a woman spat on the floor

she took a last look at the bridge
that her father had been caught blowing-up

he ate garlic susage
running amazing welcomes in his eyes

she walked through the ticket office
kissed her cousins and climbed onto the train

he kept his head down
and took another carriage

she stood in the corridor
going places

he pushed through First Class towards her
and said, It's me.

She just wanted to watch
her father's country escaping

he'd lost track

she felt trapped

trapped

Metropolitan Line

A three-pieced man is informing his wife
keeping his wife informed:
You should read on the train
in every spare minute actually
you should read everywhere
just get a book out and read it
anywhere.
You can't let the world slip by
Look at this - Obit. - a great man
very great on second thoughts
you should know about things, learn about things
staggering contribution
our society would (LIGHTS PIPE) never in one single
year
have undergone change of the sort that
popopopopopopopop ...
go on read it
sort of stuff you never read you know
actually you've pretty well gone off reading altogether
haven't you?
Come to thing of it you've even stopped talking to
people
hmmmm
what's the matter with you?

He looks out the window

LANDLADY

Mrs Porter, Polish
hoovers the stairs on Friday mornings
washes the sink on Monday
sets her front room
with photos of Krakow streets
and papers every wall with violent leaves.
She's the wife of a barren cabman
who leaves at six every morning
and eats her boiled red cabbage
when he swings home at five
in his all-white taxi.
She said the air is too wet to breathe here
and the queues in Warsaw are now long, long, long.
It is mountains that are lovely always.
She feeds me eggcupfuls of red brandy for my germs
and sits down every afternoon
in the Krakow room
to practise her exercises on the upright piano
Mr Porter played for her
in the coming of his glory.

English Literature

What fun it is to be a critic
reading poems that are anti-semitic
Eliot, Chesterton, Thackeray too
loved to write of the hateful Jew
and good old Gilbert of Sullivan fame
pitched in against the hateful same.
Cuddly Stevie Smith as well
wanted us to go to hell.
Our lives are so much the richer
for reading English Literature.

THINGS

why do people complain about easy sex?
what do they want it to be? difficult?

if someone asks you to wave the flag
they're probably stealing your bread

ever since they invented 'streetwise'
I've thought bus stops are really exciting

when I ask my brother what he does for a living
he says he's pushing back the foreskin of knowledge

whenever I look over somebody's shoulder on the
Underground
they've always got to the bit of the book where him
and her are at it

we have a free press in this country
because it's owned by free millionaires

A Moderate

His Holiness the Pope says the sun goes round the earth
while the earth goes round the sun, say extremists in the
north.
In a war of propaganda, no one says what he means
I think, the Truth, as usual, lies somewhere in between.

IN AUSTRALIA

A woman said,
some farmers round here are millionaires
but they'll come in a pub in their shorts and singlets
looking like one of the boys.
You just can't tell who's a millionaire
and who's an ordinary bloke.

I wonder if
all those men digging the roads are millionaires too.
They're wearing shorts and singlets.

Another woman told me that when she was very young
she used to sit with her brother on the gate
and watch the cars go by.
She said:
If the man and woman in the car were sitting close
together
we'd shout:
LOVERS
if they were sitting apart
we'd shout:
MARRIED.

How did we know? she said.

enough

I've heard enough about Eichmann and Himmler
Heydrick and Bormann
- sadistic maniacs etc etc
I've heard enough about Hitler
- cunning diplomacy, magnetic oratory etc etc

Just tell me
who gave them the money to start the thing off.

L.I.A.R.S

The London Institute of Applied Research Science
has discovered that there are more parks
in middle-class areas than working-class areas.
This shows, they say,
that working-class people don't like parks.

The Institute thinks that if you come from an
overcrowded home
then you should go to an overcrowded school.
If children from big spacious homes
went to overcrowded schools, they'd be very unhappy.

The Institute has discovered that none of the unemployed
who committed suicide last year, played chess.
Therefore if more unemployed people played chess
there would be fewer suicides
but then ...
If fewer unemployed people played chess
it would lower the unemployment figures.

The Institute has discovered that most women
who live at home looking after their aging mothers
don't die of AIDS, don't rob banks,
don't throw bottles at football matches, don't go on strike,
and don't blow up aeroplanes or army barracks.
The Institute concludes that everyone should stay at home
looking after their mothers.

Everyone's better off now
Everyone's better off now
except for a few thousand dossers asleep under the arches
maybe the odd prison inmate framed by a disgraced West
Midlands cop
a few thousand families in halfway hostels
going mad waiting for a flat
a few thousand women on the run from men
queueing for space in refuges
a few million in Belfast, Liverpool, London and Glasgow
in crumbling high-rise air-raid shelters
a few million dying from industrial muck
in their blood and lungs
a few million women in jobs that pay like it's Poor Relief
a few million young people walking into the brick wall
called YTS, ET or whatever
and a few million standing in the DSS
junked.

Everyone's better off now
Everyone's better off now

Politician

The politician believes in politicians,
believes that when politicians talk
it's as if it's the whole people talking.

Journalists believe in politicians.
They quote them in their papers
they keep asking them what they think
they sit them in their studios to beam their words
into our lives

they even entice real people into asking politicians
some questions
and then reverently lay their answers before us.

Out of sight of cameras
we make, we build, we celebrate, we mourn.
Throughout, we talk.
And yet we sit like galley-slaves
with our hands on the oars, not the rudder.

HANG ON

People in power, experts, say: Hang on.
Don't ask for too much, times are tough,
don't take more than you earn, hang on.

They say it this year, they said it last year,
they'll say it next year, they say it every year.

But every year, people in power, experts,
don't hang on. They live for now.

Year by year these nows become lifetimes,
How many more poor lifetimes will people put up with
before they notice it's rich lifetimes
saying, hang on, don't ask for too much
times are tough, don't take more than you earn
hang on?

Video

Rambo's great
Rambo's thrilling
Rambo's ready
Rambo's willing
war is sexy
war is fun
you got a body
I got a gun
pictures in the paper
pictures on the telly
head blown off
blasted belly
buy my video
buy my gun
you're dead
I've won
war is sexy
war is funny
war is great
war makes money
Rambo's great
Rambo's thrilling
Rambo's smiling
Rambo's killing

Families

Some people's great great great grandfathers were in
    Delhi
in September 1857.
They were with the 52nd regiment
to defeat the people called the Pandies.
When they came home, they sang:
'On the 14th of September
I remember well the date
We showed the Pandies a new hit
when we stormed the Kashmir Gate.
Their grapeshot, shell and musketry
they found but little good
when British soldiers were outside
A-thirsting for their blood.
When a-hunting we did go, my boys,
A-hunting we did go
To chase the Pandies night and day
and levelled Delhi low.'

Some people's great great grandfathers were in Kenya
at the village of Kihimbuini in September 1902.
When they came home, they said:
'We killed every living thing there, except children.
Every soul was either shot or bayoneted.
We burned all the huts and razed the banana plantation
to the ground.'

Great grandfathers were in St Johnston, Leewards
Islands,

In the West Indies in January 1936.
When they came home, they said:
'We moved in on a sugar cane estate.
There was a march with a drummer at its head.
Our commanding officer read them the Riot Act,
then we fired our rifles at them. About three of them
    died.'

Grandfathers were in Malaya in August 1948.
When they came home, they said:
'We told the villagers to get out. We burnt down their
    huts
and we took the men of the village to a camp.
There were thousands of them in there. Some from
Pulai.
Pulai was bombed by the RAF the month before.'

Fathers were in Derry, Ireland, in January 1972.
When they came home, they said:
'Some of the marchers were trying to get out
of the Rossville Flats Car Park into Joseph Place.
As they came through between the blocks of flats
we let them have it. We saw two go down.'

Boys were outside Hashamua Patel's grocery store
in Tooting, London in June 1983.
When they came home, they said:
'We lit the rag and threw the bomb at their shop
    window.'

Welcome

Welcome to the museum
First we'd like to show you round the Dress Collection.
Here you can look at the clothes:
dresses, shoes, hats, coats and so on
worn for the last 400 years
by rich shits.
We feel that only these clothes
should be the ones on view
because everything that rich shits do
is much more important than anything that you do.
No one wants to see the kinds of things worn by
harvesters, pregnant women, seamen, prisoners, weavers,
mill girls and plough boys.
And in the glass case meant for modern fashion
you won't be seeing teds and hippies and skin heads.
They're not art.
I'm afraid there isn't room for the outfits
worn by
Bengalis, Jews, Africans and Caribbeans in Britain today
because that isn't English dress, is it?
We only have room for that kind of thing
in the galleries reserved for the loot of the British Empire.
So come over here and admire something worn by
some rich creep at James I's court

probably making his money
out of kicking people off common land
and saying it belonged to him.
Move along a bit and see a few Regency drones
wrapped in silk
woven by starving weavers in Lyon.
And if you cut across to here
you can see a row of fat flowery ties
worn by sixties admen and media slugs.
It's art.

some rich creeps . . .

BANK

At Bank Station
when the doors of the train open
a recording of a deep hollowy man's voice
slowly says:
MIND THE GAP

It sounds like he's talking down a drain.
It's the only thing he can say, you know.
When he gets home at night
his kids say:
Have a nice day at work, Dad?
He says:
MIND THE GAP

His wife says:
Do you want to watch TV?
he says:
MIND THE GAP

And later
after the kids have gone to bed
she says:
Darling, do you still love me?
and he says:
MIND THE GAP

Look at me

Look at me, I go to school
do as I'm told, don't play the fool

work like crazy, never slack
smile all the time, don't answer back

all right, I know, I'm not all that bright,
but I get by, doing what's right

lot of others, mess about
every night, they're off out
getting into fights, acting tough
on the streets, nicking stuff.

One thing bothers me, been on my mind,
nearly finished at school, breaking up time,

looking for a job, doing the rounds
knocking on doors, all over town

the others don't bother, of course that's why
they don't get jobs ... but why don't I?

And funny thing too, I'm like my dad
he's never done wrong, never been bad

never has a day off, does more than his whack
but only last week, he got the sack.

Makes me think, doesn't matter what you do,
in the end, they try and do it to you.

money

I love the ads
they're really funny
telling you to buy
when you not got the money

get a telly
get a toaster
get a cooker
get a motor

if you ain't got the money, it's OK, borrow
use a bank card, clear it tomorrow

that's what you do, buy all the stuff
few weeks later, it gets a bit rough

watching the telly, some rainy day
bill arrives, oh shit, can't pay.

I love the ads
they're really funny
telling you to buy
when you not got the money

get a telly
get a toaster
get a cooker
get a motor

None of this matters, the bank manager said,
borrow what you like, so long as you're not dead.

Clever bugger knows he's got me on the rack
every pound I borrow he gets a 10p extra back

he doesn't care, I could be 95
so long as I'm working and still alive

I love the ads
they're really funny
telling you to buy
when you not got the money

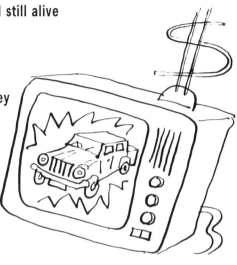

get a telly
get a toaster
get a cooker
get a motor

get a debt
get the sack
get no money
to pay it back

bloke on the telly
says face life with a grin
small wonder some
do themselves in

Small wonder some
don't keep quiet
small wonder some
start a riot

I love the ads
they're really funny
telling you to buy
when you not got the money

snog her 742 1534

I used to sit by the phone
and dare myself to ring her.
I once dialled the number
and when someone picked the phone up
the other end
I put the phone down.

Then it was Christmas
and Mr P put mistletoe up
over the classroom door,
and one night after school
there was only me, her and her friend Diane.
I'm standing there getting my stuff
and she goes and grabs the mistletoe
and starts walking towards me.
She's got the mistletoe in her hand
and she's looking at me
with her eyes all dark in the middle
and when she gets to me she says:
'You know what they do under the mistletoe,
don't you?'
And she's in really close to me
and so our two faces move towards each other

and something like a kiss started happening.
It was all spongey
and I'm thinking: I suppose this is all for Diane's benefit
the others'll all come in in a minute
or maybe Mr P
and then it'll all be a
Big Deal
about snogging in school ...

... and suddenly she says:
'Well open your mouth then.
You can't kiss with your mouth shut.
You need much more experience,
still, I've got to go now, come on, Diane.
Happy Christmas,
bye.'

742 1534

snog

END OF THE WORLD

The papers said
that people were saying
it was going to be
THE END OF THE WORLD
Wednesday, dinner time.

Ken and Monkee and the rest
said we ought to have an
END OF THE WORLD CEREMONY
so we went out there
in front of school
on the East Field
where there was
NO RUNNING
NO BALL GAMES
NO SHOUTING
AND BOYS AND GIRLS MUST BE
AT LEAST THREE FEET APART
AT ALL TIMES.

and we whipped our shirts off
put our jackets over our heads
rolled our trouser legs up
and started singing:
The End of the World is Coming
hoob de hoob
de hoob-hoob-hoob
oh woh, oh woh
wailing
whooping
and jiving about.

hoob de hoob
de hoob-hoob-hoob

80

So hundreds of kids
came crowding round
and we gave it everything we had:
hoob de hoob
repent repent
the end is nigh
half the school was queuing up

and then the whistles started blowing
teachers were bursting out of doors
and motoring towards us
at nine million miles per hour.
It was the snatch squad.

Monkee knew what to do:
'Brothers and sisters
follow me to the
END OF THE WORLD', he shouts
and we whopped off to the toilets
like it was the end of the world or something.

Nothing else happened
even though we had disturbed the peace
made an affray
and committed riotous and disorderly acts
on the East Field.

Though on my report
at the end of term
the head wrote:
I don't mind him
celebrating the end of the old world
I hope he enters the new one
a little more soberly.

hoob de hoob
de hoob-hoob-hoob

81

Cullen

If you ever wanted to know

what this guy Cullen was doing

he didn't tell you to sod off

he didn't say, get your nose out of it,

what's it to you?

he just said:

Trunk out,

you heard, trunk out.

I haven't seen him for 25 years.

I think he lectures in Economics

at Birmingham University now.

THE OTHERS

The others once said to me
why don't you come with us
up to Grantham House?
- No I don't think so, I said.
We're going at night
and we climb over the gate
and go into the woods
by the side of the house,
are you coming?
- No I don't think so.
And then we wait
and watch the house
because every night
one of the patients
comes to the window,
are you coming?
- No I don't think so.
And she's starkers
she cleans the windows
all the windows
one after the other
starkers
are you coming?
- No I don't think so.
But you see everything,
go on, come with us,
what do you say?
- No I don't think so.

Notes on spitting,
(gobbing, flobbing)

men do it
teenage boys do it
women don't do it
girls don't do it

spitting is therefore
male
and grown up

this means it's probably
genetic
like eye-colour
and finger-prints
boys inherit spitting from fathers
but because it starts happening
at about 11
it's like growing a moustache,
chest hairs, etc
ie secondary sex characteristic.
Spitting is
a secondary sex characteristic
missing from text books
on facts of life, sex education,
how to do it, etc
(make note to write to
'How You were Made'
'All You Ever Wanted to Know About Sex'
'Dr Dick Answers All Your Questions'
telling them about this discovery)

To continue:
Primary sex characteristics
are useful:
they are fun and make babies
Secondary sex characteristics
are not as useful or as fun.
They are tiring as
they need looking after
(beards, armpits etc)
and people get them wrong:
eg: 'That guy looks like a girl'
or 'That girl looks like a guy'.

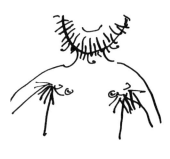

Spitting
is a true secondary sex characteristic
because it too is not useful
and people get it wrong:
(mess down jacket,
blowback out of train windows, etc)

Proposal:
ban secondary sex characteristics
so bye bye pubic hair etc
and bye bye spitting in my road
(a major world spitting centre,
people from all over the British Isles
come there to spit)

Conclusion:
Razor firms may go out of business,
but I won't skid on the way to the bus stop.

PLAQUES

You who love history
you who love heroes
you who want to know about Great Men and Women
come to the walls of houses and palaces
and read the names of artists, reformers, inventors,
leaders, statesmen and entertainers.

You who were not great
when death was the meaning of your life
can find your names in the long lists on war
memorials.
They found room for you there.
But there is no room on the vast grey walls of new
blocks,
station forecourts, motorway piers or multi-storey car
parks
for the names of those who died on the sites.

Occasional national frenzy over mining disasters,
train crashes, and aeroplane explosions
fills the front pages.
A Royal death unites us in mourning
with grief-stricken polo players and multi-millionaire
show-jumpers
and their tears drown the sound of a bricklayer
tripping on a scaffold-plank and landing on his spine.

For him
no plaque.

He said:

People!
Listen to what I say
(people do listen to what I say
people have to listen to what I say)
you are going to listen to what I say
you know you will have to listen to what I
say
(but you do not know that what you listen
to me saying
is all garbage)

HOW HE DIDN'T TELL HER THAT HE WAS SEEING SOMEONE ELSE:

she rings and says: hi it's me, you didn't ring

no

so I'm ringing

right

is there anywhere you wanted to go, tonight?

no not really

is that why you didn't ring?

sort of

you mean you didn't want to ring?

I wasn't going to say that

you didn't want to ring though, did you?

I dunno

so what am I supposed to do? hang around waiting for a call

88

I didn't say that

what are you saying?

nothing much

is anything wrong?

no no no

*I'll ring you when
you're in a better mood.*

right

shall I?

sure

*don't sound so pleased
about it*

right

bye ter-rah

NOTES ON AiDS
(NB NOT AIDS,
BUT LIVE AID ETC)

poor countries need Aid
because they are poor

They are poor because
they have no money

Because they have no money
they have no food

Now some questions:

Why don't they grow food?
Because they are growing coffee, tea, etc

Can they eat coffee tea etc?
No

Why are they growing coffee?
To get money.

Do they get the money?
No they give the money to us

And then they buy the food?
No the money is ours, they owe it to us

90

You mean they borrowed money?
Yep.

To buy food?
No, to grow coffee, tea, etc.

Why did they do that?
We told them to

Why did we do that?
So that they could be modern.

Are they modern?
No, they can't afford to be.

Last question:
Who is 'we'?
Banks.

Conclusion:
They grow coffee, tea, etc
pay banks money
starve.

Proposal:
Short cut: next Live Aid to be not for Ethiopia
etc
but for banks ... ie Bank Aid

Malc

If you wanted to sound
really big
or really flash
then you could say you'd been
up to London
on your own
up the West End.

You had to talk about it
like you knew where the best record shops were
and where you could get
really good spaghetti bolognaise
really cheap.

So me and my friend Malc
we arranged to go up to London
on our own
up the West End
I'd already been with my older brother
and his friends

so I knew about Dobells Jazz record shop
Jimmy's Bar in the basement in Greek Street
and the 100 club.

I reckoned I could sound
really big
really flash
and cool with it.

Me and Malc met up
at Westminster Station
next to the Houses of Parliament and Big Ben.
We went over to a street map
that was on one of those roller things
and we rolled through the maps:
London's Car Parks
Where to find the statues.

We start to plan
where we would go.
I say:
We could mosey up Whitehall to Charing Cross
Road
and do Dobells Jazz Shop.
Yeah, says Malc.
And then we could move on down Wardour
Street
and take in the movie posters, I say.
Yeah, says Malc.

Then I say:
What's the time?
Dunno, says Malc, haven't got a watch.
Neither have I, I say.

There was a man standing next to us.
I can handle this, I thought.
I can look a stranger in the eye
and ask him the time
when I'm up the West End.

Leave this to me, Malc, OK? Mmmmm?

Excuse me, I said,
Have you go the time?

The man looked at me,
waved his hands and said:
Deutsch.

I stopped for a moment.
Deutsch? Deutsch?
He's German
Huh
that's no problem
I can handle this one too.
I've done a year of German at School
I know my way about
International London.

Leave this to me, Malc, OK? Mmmmm

And I turn to the man
and say:
Wie viel uhr ist es
(what's the time, in German)

The man looked at me again
and then very slowly
he
looked
up

and pointed.

We looked up too

there was Big Ben

the whole world
knows that Big Ben tells the time
and there I was
standing underneath the damn thing
asking a German bloke
what's the time?

The man said:
I thought you were asking me that
to laugh at me.

I was going all red and hot and flustered
and Malcolm
he was cracked up all over the place
laughing his head off at me.

Now anytime I meet Malc
and he thinks
I'm trying to sound
really big
really flash
and cool with it
he says: Mike?
Yeah?
Wie viel uhr ist es?

INDEX